For Rob Weisbach

KOUT

BY JOHN ROCCO

Disney • Hyperion Books
New York

IT STARTED OUT AS A NORMAL SUMMER NIGHT.

THE CITY WAS LOUD AND HOT.

INSIDE, EVERYONE WAS BUSY.

AND THEN . . .

THE LIGHTS

WENT

OUT.

NOTHING WORKED AT ALL.

AND STILL.

WE HUDDLED AROUND FLASHLIGHTS
AND CANDLES . . .

... UNTIL IT WAS TOO HOT
AND STICKY TO SIT INSIDE.

TO THE ROOFTOP

AND
FOUND . . .

THE LIGHTS.

AND PEOPLE!
IT WAS A BLOCK PARTY
IN THE SKY.

WE WAVED TO EVERYONE,
THEN HEARD OTHER SOUNDS BELOW.

So we went down

and down

and down

WHEN THE LIGHTS CAME BACK ON,

EVERYTHING WENT BACK TO NORMAL . . .

CLICK

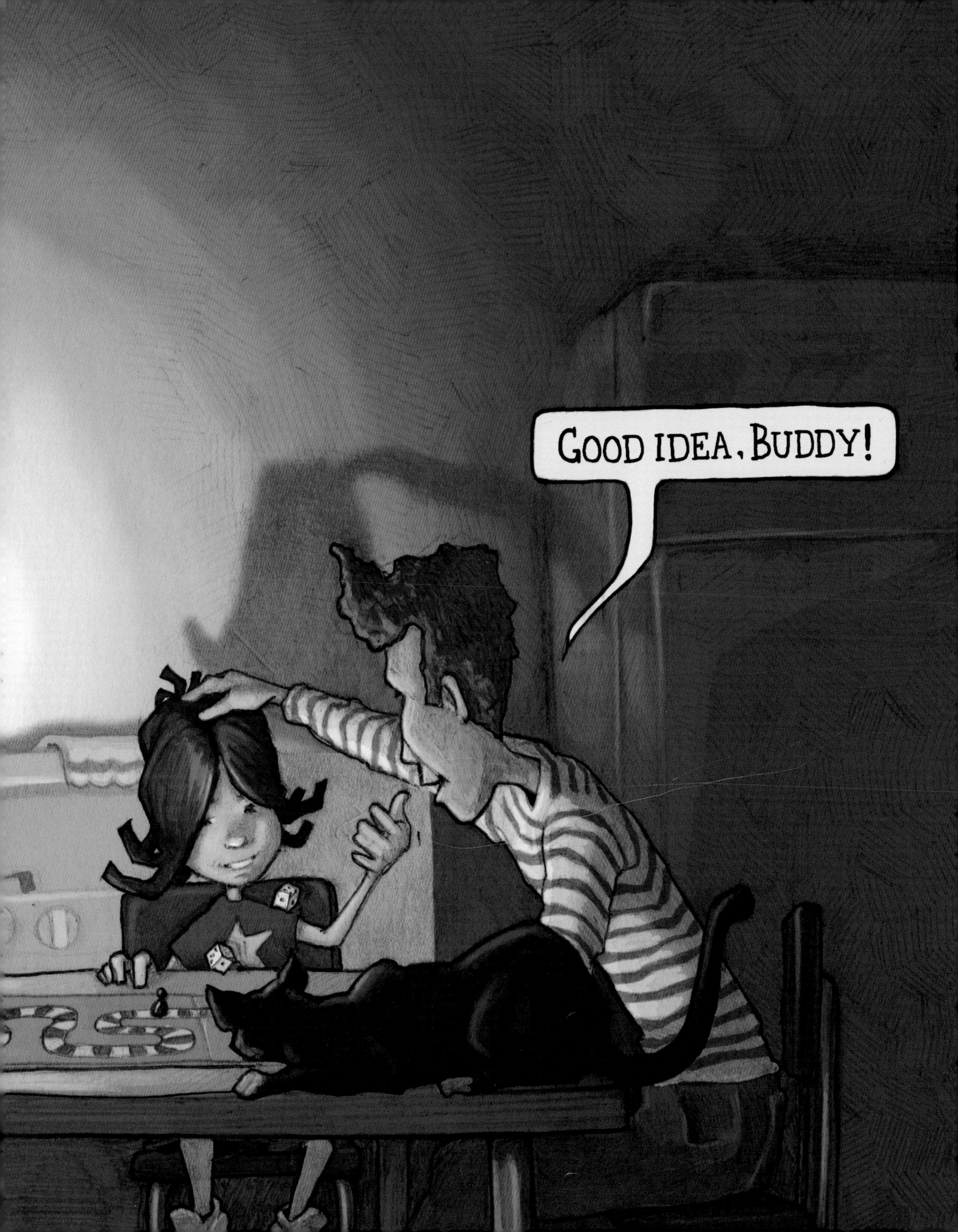
GOOD IDEA, BUDDY!

THE END